From the Films of

Harry Potter ™

EXPLORING HOGWARTS

An Illustrated Guide

Text by Jody Revenson

Illustrations by Studio Muti

INSIGHT
EDITIONS

SAN RAFAEL • LOS ANGELES • LONDON

Dear Reader,

We are pleased to invite you on a tour of Hogwarts School of Witchcraft and Wizardry.

Within these pages, you'll explore Hogwarts castle as seen in the Harry Potter films, from its talking portraits and moving staircases to its tallest towers and deepest dungeons. You'll even enter into the Forbidden Forest with Harry Potter and gamekeeper Rubeus Hagrid, and come upon centaurs, Thestrals, and an Acromantula the size of an elephant!

Along the way, you'll relive beloved moments from the films, and learn secrets about the movie magic used to bring this thousand-year-old castle to life on-screen. Even if you've seen the Harry Potter films dozens of times, there's still much to discover inside.

So, as Hagrid says in Harry Potter and the Sorcerer's Stone, "Right, then, this way to the boats! Follow me!"

HOGWARTS SCHOOL of WITCHCRAFT & WIZARDRY
Headmaster: Albus Dumbledore, D.Wiz., X.J.(sorc.), S.of Mag.Q.

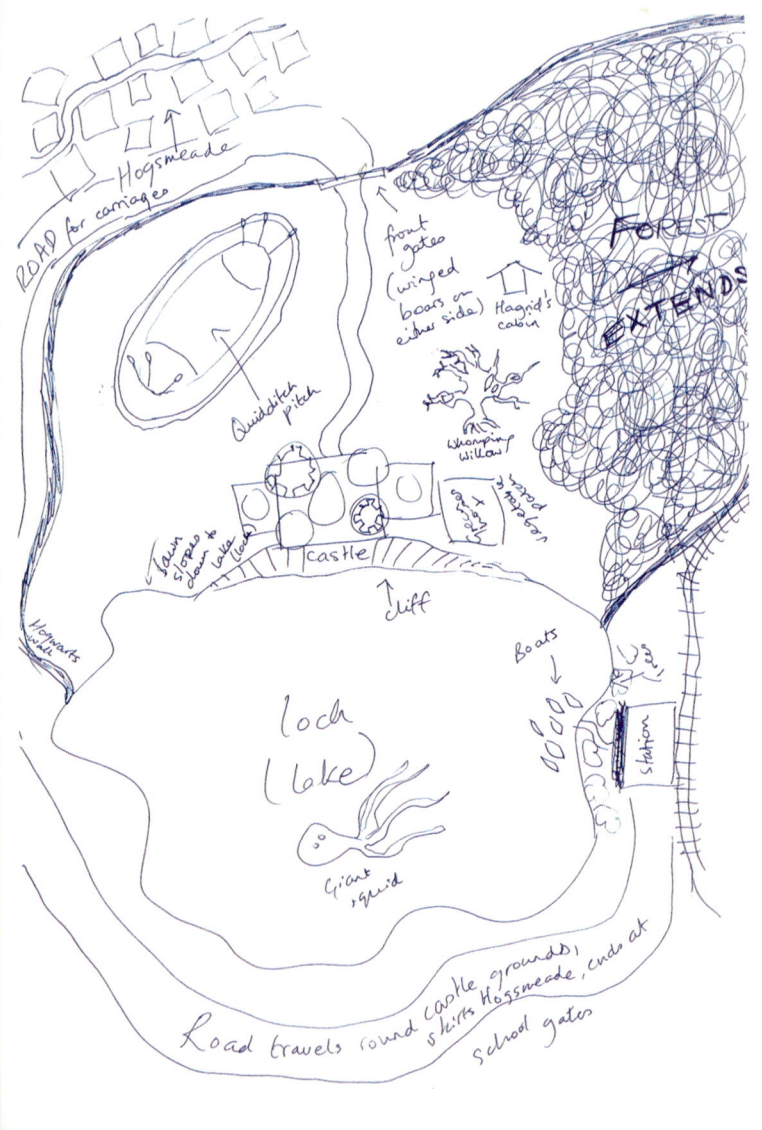

Hogsmeade

ROAD for carriages

front gates
(winged
boars on
either side)

FOREST

EXTENDS

Hagrid's
cabin

Quidditch pitch

Whomping
Willow

wood + water
station

Lawn slopes
down to
lake (loch)

castle

cliff

Boats

station

Hogwarts
wall

loch
(lake)

Giant
squid

Road travels round castle grounds,
skirts Hogsmeade, ends at
school gates

When production designer Stuart Craig was brought aboard to bring the story of Harry Potter and his adventures to the movie screen, he went to the source—author J. K. Rowling—with a list of questions about Hogwarts castle and its surroundings—the Forbidden Forest, the Black Lake, and even the Whomping Willow.

Immediately, Rowling drew him a map that illustrated how the castle was situated, where the Quidditch pitch was located, and how Hogwarts students made their way from the Hogsmeade train station to the school. Craig considered that map the ultimate authority and pinned it above his drawing table, where it stayed for ten years of filming.

The Forbidden Forest

The Owle

Hagrid's
Hut

The Shrieking
Shack

The Great
Hall

The Quidditch Pitch

Hogsmeade

Hogsmeade Station

The
Whomping
Willow

adore's
Office

The Black Lake

The
Boathouse

9

HOGWARTS CASTLE,
PART I

First-year students arrive in small boats that sail over the **Black Lake**, giving them their first view of Hogwarts castle in *Harry Potter and the Sorcerer's Stone*.

Many scenes in *Sorcerer's Stone* and *Harry Potter and the Chamber of Secrets* were shot at locations that inspired the castle's architecture.

These locations were later recreated at the film studio, which gave Stuart Craig an opportunity to revise his original design. Craig felt that a magical castle could believably change over time.

For *Chamber of Secrets*, the Defense Against the Dark Arts classroom (originally shot on location in the **Warming Room** in Lacock Abbey, England) and Albus Dumbledore's office were assigned to towers that were already part of the Hogwarts silhouette in the first movie.

Hogwarts School of Witchcraft and Wizardry is a one-thousand-year-old educational institution, so Stuart Craig looked at the great British universities and cathedrals from the same era for the castle's design. Craig felt that if the towers and halls seemed familiar, not fairy tale–like, the magic would appear even more real.

Harry Potter and the Prisoner of Azkaban saw the most revisions to the design of Hogwarts, as director Alfonso Cuarón wanted connectivity between key locations. New story elements required the addition of towers and sites for new classrooms. Other changes included moving Hagrid's hut further away from the castle.

With the theme of time running throughout the *Prisoner of Azkaban* story, the tall **Clock Tower** was added to the back of the castle. On its lower level, the clock's pendulum swung back and forth before the entrance to a small courtyard.

DID YOU NOTICE?

The new **courtyard** surrounded a central fountain decorated with serpents and eagles. These creatures, from the Mexican coat of arms, were a reference to Cuarón's heritage.

HOGWARTS CASTLE,
PART II

An **Owlery** was added for *Harry Potter and the Goblet of Fire*. Set a ways from the castle, the Owlery is a tall, cylindrical tower filled with windows perched on an equally tall rock. The design was a mash-up of French pigeon coops called *pigeonniers* and stately British houses.

As the film series progressed, Hogwarts castle continued to gain and lose towers. Its entrances were enlarged, and elements were shifted around in the grounds. Stuart Craig admitted that it would have been nice to read through all seven Harry Potter books before filming started. But he also felt that the changes added a level of interest to the films.

Voldemort and his snake, Nagini, confronted Severus Snape in a redesigned Gothic boathouse in *Deathly Hallows – Part 2*. Its walls of windows glowed with reflections of fires that burned at Hogwarts castle.

At the end of *Half-Blood Prince*, Dumbledore has died and Harry is left with what he thinks is the real **Slytherin Locket**. Harry and Hermione stand on the tower and open it, only to discover that it is a fake and that the real Horcrux is missing.

The biggest change in the castle in *Half-Blood Prince* was the addition of the **Astronomy Tower**. It replaced the Defense Against the Dark Arts Tower and became the tallest structure at Hogwarts.

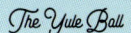

The Yule Ball

For the Triwizard Tournament's Yule Ball in *Goblet of Fire,* the entrance to the Great Hall needed to be lowered to ground level to accommodate carriages arriving and dropping off students. In the early films, this entryway was shot on location at Christ Church College at Oxford University, but it was very small, so the entryway was recreated at the film studio.

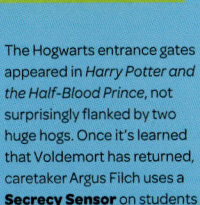

The Hogwarts entrance gates appeared in *Harry Potter and the Half-Blood Prince,* not surprisingly flanked by two huge hogs. Once it's learned that Voldemort has returned, caretaker Argus Filch uses a **Secrecy Sensor** on students entering the gates to locate any security breaches.

Luna Lovegood fixes Harry's broken nose with *Episkey* as they enter the gates.

🎬 For *Harry Potter and the Deathly Hallows – Part 2,* a larger stone viaduct bridge was added that led directly from the entrance courtyard, which itself was enlarged to accommodate the Battle of Hogwarts and the final duel between Harry and Voldemort.

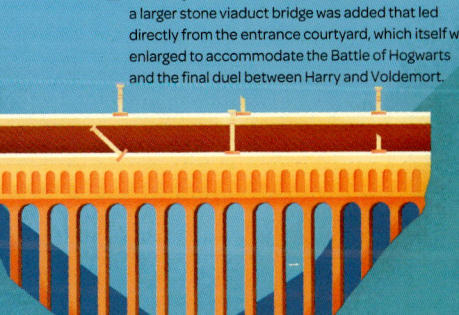

MOVING STAIRCASES AND TALKING PORTRAITS

Within Hogwarts is a square spiral of staircases that reaches up endlessly. The stairs not only connect to platforms leading in each compass direction, they can also *move*—sometimes when least expected—creating new ways of getting around the castle.

> "OH, AND KEEP AN EYE ON THE STAIRS . . . THEY LIKE TO CHANGE."
>
> **Percy Weasley**,
> *Harry Potter and the Sorcerer's Stone*

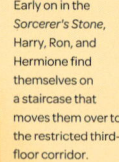

Early on in the *Sorcerer's Stone*, Harry, Ron, and Hermione find themselves on a staircase that moves them over to the restricted third-floor corridor.

🎬 Stuart Craig had to first figure out *how* the staircases moved. An early thought was to treat them like escalators. Then Craig came up with the idea that any one staircase could swing ninety degrees to a new position. So, a staircase placed against one wall could move to create a bridge to the opposite wall. This intertwined coil of the **Grand Staircase**, created digitally, forms a double helix.

DID YOU NOTICE?

There were 350 portraits on the walls of Hogwarts castle, 200 of them on the Grand Staircase. While many of them were static pictures, a good number interacted with the students.

In *Prisoner of Azkaban*, the escaped prisoner—Sirius Black—tries to break into the Gryffindor common room. In fear, many of the paintings' subjects run from frame to frame, including the **Fat Lady**, who finds safety in a portrait of a small hippopotamus. Creating movement between the works of art was complicated, as the scale of the paintings varied greatly.

A scene with moving or talking portraits would be filmed with green-screen material in the picture frames. The background for the portrait would be painted and scanned into the computer. Then actors or crew members were filmed in front of a green screen, and all these elements were digitally combined.

Argus Filch was ordered by headmistress Dolores Umbridge to remove the portraits from the walls in *Harry Potter and the Order of the Phoenix*.

In *Deathly Hallows – Part 2*, the portraits were recreated with empty backgrounds after their subjects had fled for safety from the battle.

LIBRARY

Wearing his **Invisibility Cloak**, Harry Potter snuck into the Restricted Section of the Library in *Sorcerer's Stone* to find information on Nicolas Flamel, the only known maker of the Sorcerer's Stone, which grants immortality.

🎬 The Library scenes in *Sorcerer's Stone* were shot at Duke Humfrey's Library at Oxford University. This library chained its oldest books to a frame inside the bookshelves.

Among the many books at the Hogwarts Library are tomes about fantastic beasts, self-defense spell work, great wizards, healing plants, and the history of magic. Students use the Library for homework help, a quiet space, and sometimes research into subjects they shouldn't be studying!

Eleven thousand books were created for the Library, many of which were actually covered phone books. Towers of books were stacked on the floors, and some even floated through the air. These airborne books were made of lightweight Styrofoam.

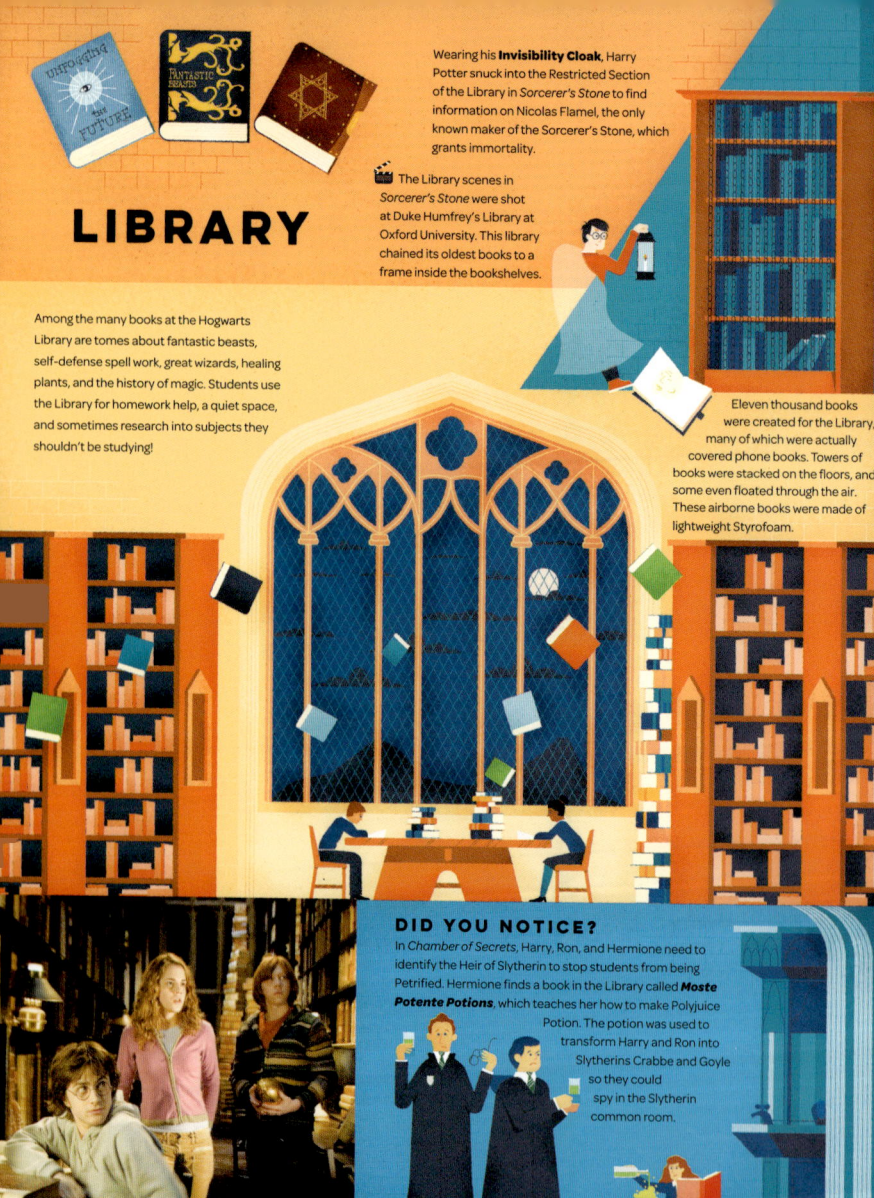

DID YOU NOTICE?

In *Chamber of Secrets*, Harry, Ron, and Hermione need to identify the Heir of Slytherin to stop students from being Petrified. Hermione finds a book in the Library called ***Moste Potente Potions***, which teaches her how to make Polyjuice Potion. The potion was used to transform Harry and Ron into Slytherins Crabbe and Goyle so they could spy in the Slytherin common room.

In *Goblet of Fire*, Harry, Ron, and Hermione search in the Library to find something to help Harry with the Triwizard Tournament's second task under the waters of the Black Lake. It's Neville Longbottom who suggests **Gillyweed**, which he discovered in a herbology book.

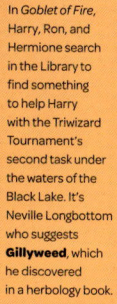

As Hermione vents her frustrations about Ron Weasley to Harry in the *Half-Blood Prince*, she restacks books—some of which appear to float up to their shelves. Crew members wearing green-screen gloves reached through the stacks and grabbed the lightweight books from her hands.

Graphic designers Miraphora Mina and Eduardo Lima led a team that created all the books. They learned techniques of bookmaking, like creating covers out of metal and gold leaf. Books that were seen on-screen up close were created in at least two sizes—one for the student to hold and a larger version for close-ups. Every book contained twenty pages of hand-drawn or printed material created by the graphic designers that was repeated over and over.

GREAT HALL

The Great Hall is where Hogwarts students study, receive mail from home, eat meals, and celebrate. Arguably the most iconic setting in the Harry Potter films, the Great Hall set was used for nearly ten years of filming.

"IT'S NOT REAL, THE CEILING. IT'S JUST BEWITCHED."

Hermione Granger,
Harry Potter and the Sorcerer's Stone

Hundreds of **magical candles** float above the student tables, lighting up the Hall. The candles became digital after several real candles fell during the first filming of the Sorting scene.

The House Cup

Every year, the four Hogwarts houses compete for the House Cup, which is awarded to the house that has earned the most points. Professors award points for actions that reflect well on the house, such as academic achievement or bravery. Hourglasses in the Great Hall keep track of which house is in the lead- and which have fallen behind.

The Sorting Hat

Before the first feast of the school year, first-year students are sorted into one of four houses: Gryffindor, Hufflepuff, Ravenclaw, or Slytherin. The Sorting Hat in *Sorcerer's Stone* was a combination of leather hat prop placed on their heads and a computer-generated talking hat that announced their house. There were seven leather hats created for the films, each with slightly different wrinkles, but since you never see them together, you'd never know!

DID YOU NOTICE?

The Great Hall's ceiling is bewitched to mirror the weather outside of Hogwarts. The **enchanted ceiling** is seen only once during the daytime in the Harry Potter films: When Fred and George Weasley set off fireworks during the fifth-year O.W.L. exams, the sky is blue and dotted with a few clouds.

Each house has its own **resident ghost**, who lives in and out of the Great Hall. Ravenclaw has the Grey Lady; Hufflepuff, the Fat Friar; and Slytherin, the Bloody Baron. Gryffindor's ghost is Sir Nicholas de Mimsy-Porpington, or Nearly Headless Nick.

The actors were encouraged to write their names on the tables, just as real students might.

The Great Hall is 40 feet by 120 feet and is often furnished with **four 90-foot-long tables**- one for each of the school's houses.

DEFENSE AGAINST THE DARK ARTS CLASSROOMS

In Defense Against the Darks Arts class, students are taught how to protect and defend themselves against dangerous spells, deadly curses, and menacing creatures. It proved difficult to hold onto a professor for this class over the course of the story, so each new school year, the Defense Against the Dark Arts classroom was redecorated to reflect the new teacher.

DID YOU NOTICE? Books authored by **Gilderoy Lockhart** and moving photos depicting his "adventures" decorated his classroom. During his first class, he exchanged a wink with a moving portrait of himself—which was painting a portrait of himself!

Professor Quirrell's classroom was filmed on location in Lacock Abbey's dungeonlike thirteenth-century Warming Room for the *Sorcerer's Stone*.

Starting with *Chamber of Secrets*, a classroom was constructed in the studio that had one curved wall and was set at the top of a tower. Tall windows on one side of the attic-type room flooded the area with light. The classroom held eighteen double desks. As the actors grew, the desks needed to be replaced with bigger versions.

Third-year professor **Remus Lupin** taught his students to use the *Riddikulus* Spell against **Boggarts**, which turn into your worst fear. Using *Riddikulus*, Neville Longbottom dressed Boggart Professor Snape in his grandmother's clothes and hat, and Ron turned the Boggart from a scary spider to one wearing eight roller skates.

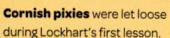
Cornish pixies were let loose during Lockhart's first lesson.

 The Defense Against the Dark Arts professor in *Goblet of Fire*, **Alastor "Mad-Eye" Moody**, had a magical eye that inspired set designer Stephenie McMillan to decorate the classroom with huge glass lenses and other optometric-type equipment. Moody taught a lesson on the three Unforgiveable Curses using a spider made huge by the Engorgement Charm.

A Gothic-style pulpit sits atop stairs that lead to the professor's office. Stuart Craig felt it would be a great theatrical entrance for the second-year Defense Against the Dark Arts professor, Gilderoy Lockhart, in *Chamber of Secrets*.

Dolores Umbridge, the professor in *Order of the Phoenix*, didn't believe in teaching her students defensive magic, so her classroom was left plain. The textbook she chose floated to each student's desk.

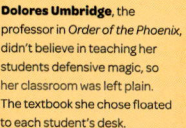

PROFESSORS' OFFICES

The office of each Hogwarts professor also reflected his or her personality or passions. Though the Defense Against the Dark Arts office lacked identity, as it housed a new professor each year, the other offices became a home away from home for their resident professors.

Severus Snape's Office

In *Chamber of Secrets*, Harry Potter and Ron Weasley are brought to the Potions Master's office after they crash a flying car into the Whomping Willow. The small, cramped room was filled with hundreds of hand-labeled jars containing potions ingredients, and very little else.

Gilderoy Lockhart's Office

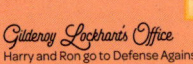

Harry and Ron go to Defense Against the Dark Arts Professor Gilderoy Lockhart's office to ask for his help with the Chamber of Secrets, and they discover the professor packing to leave Hogwarts! Large trunks and bags held his extensive wardrobe and photos of himself.

Horace Slughorn's Office

When he returned to teach Potions at Hogwarts in the *Half-Blood Prince*, Horace Slughorn insisted on having a large, comfortable office. The set was a redesign of the Room of Requirement filled with large, brown leather sofas and a dining table where he could entertain members of the **Slug Club**.

Slughorn had his own purple-lined trunk, which held potions ingredients. The antique was filled with hand-labeled bottles and boxes. Fortunately, one contained a Bezoar, which Harry used as an antidote to save a poisoned Ron Weasley.

Remus Lupin's Office

Remus Lupin's steamer trunk packed itself at the end of *Prisoner of Azkaban* when the beloved teacher left the school. Pulleys and electric motors pulled loose books and shoes into their compartments, closed drawers, and pulled Lupin's jacket inside the threadbare antique case.

 Lupin returns the Marauder's Map—which shows the location of everyone at Hogwarts—to Harry, closing it with a tap. The refolding of the map to its closed position was actually achieved with a practical effect using thread.

Alastan Moody's Office

Fourth-year Defense Against the Dark Arts professor, Alastor "Mad-Eye" Moody's office held a Foe-Glass, a Dark Detector that allowed him to see if his enemies were sneaking up on him.

In *Goblet of Fire*, it's discovered that the Defense Against the Dark Arts teacher is actually the Polyjuice-potioned **Death Eater Barty Crouch Jr.** The real Moody is concealed in a trunk in the office. The mechanical trunk could raise its seven compartments one at a time, from the largest to the smallest.

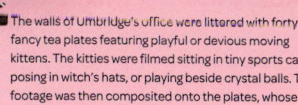 The walls of Umbridge's office were littered with forty fancy tea plates featuring playful or devious moving kitties. The kitties were filmed sitting in tiny sports cars, posing in witch's hats, or playing beside crystal balls. This footage was then composited onto the plates, whose centers had been colored with a bright green paint.

Dolores Umbridge's Office

The office of Harry's Defense Against the Dark Arts professor in *Order of the Phoenix* was in sharp contrast to her empty, dark classroom. Dolores Umbridge's office was painted pink, with pink drapes, a pink carpet, pink furniture, and pink everything!

HOGWARTS GROUNDS AND THE BLACK LAKE

Set beside a large lake and a forbidden forest, the Hogwarts grounds offer places to take broom-flying classes, play the favorite wizarding sport, Quidditch, or hide tunnels that lead away from the castle.

The covered wooden bridge was extended for *Deathly Hallows – Part 2*. Neville Longbottom and Seamus Finnigan blew up the bridge in an effort to stop Voldemort's army of Death Eaters and Snatchers.

A large freshwater body of water called the **Black Lake** shimmers beside Hogwarts castle. Buckbeak the Hippogriff skimmed his talons in its murky waters when Harry rode him in the *Prisoner of Azkaban*.

The version of Buckbeak that walked and flew was digital.

When Harry and Ron miss the Hogwarts Express in *Chamber of Secrets*, they drive Arthur Weasley's flying Ford Anglia car to school. Ron crashes it into a **Whomping Willow** on the broom-training grounds. The eighty-five-foot tree, which swallows up the car, was constructed in two parts, with rubber-coated mechanical branches that whomped the car until it was spit out.

In *Prisoner of Azkaban*, the Whomping Willow was moved closer to the castle so it was in a better position to provide an entrance to a tunnel that led to the **Shrieking Shack** in Hogsmeade. The tree's base was also changed to accommodate students and professors going in and out. Computer-generated branches were added to the mechanical ones for even more whomping.

The Stone Circle

The circle of five large stones is reminiscent of British henges, such as Stonehenge.

Hermione Granger punched Draco Malfoy in the stone circle after he laughed at Hagrid's grief when Buckbeak the Hippogriff was sentenced to die.

A path led down the hill from the stone circle to Hagrid's hut, which gained a second room and a pumpkin patch in *Prisoner of Azkaban*. For the *Half-Blood Prince*, the stone circle was moved to the other side of Hagrid's hut, and the Quidditch pitch was moved closer to the wooden bridge.

The **Durmstrang students** arrived in a ship that surfaced from underneath the waters of the Black Lake in the *Goblet of Fire*.

Since the **Quidditch pitch** would have been too big to build on a soundstage or on location in Scotland, it was an almost entirely digital set.

The broom-flying class led by **Madam Hooch** in *Sorcerer's Stone* was filmed on location at Alnwick Castle.

THE FORBIDDEN FOREST

A dark, thick forest surrounds several sides of Hogwarts castle. For good reason, Albus Dumbledore tells first-year students they are forbidden to go there in *Sorcerer's Stone*. Many of the creatures that reside there are not friendly.

The forest was filmed on location for the first film, then created in a studio for each film thereafter. To "make" the forest, tree trunks were constructed and hung above the set. Then carved roots were set into the stage floor, and the trunks were attached to these.

Harry, Ron, Hermione, and Draco serve detention in the forest in *Sorcerer's Stone*, accompanied by Hagrid and his cowardly dog, **Fang**. The forest floor was covered in moss to protect the feet of the canine actor who played Fang.

Harry met the centaur **Firenze** in *Sorcerer's Stone*.

Stuart Craig decided that the farther one got into the forest, the bigger, creepier, and more mysterious it would become. As the films progressed, the trees became bigger and bigger, and they were perched on massive roots that looked like fingers, based on mangrove trees. Even the mist used to add a layer of hazy fog became thicker in the later films.

For *Prisoner of Azkaban*, the forest was recreated with a real frozen lake, where Harry and Sirius encountered Dementors. Actors Daniel Radcliffe and Gary Oldman worked with black-cloaked puppets before digital Dementors were added.

In *Chamber of Secrets*, Harry and Ron travel to a hollow where a colony of Acromantula spiders live, headed by their king, **Aragog**. The king of the spiders built by the creature shop, had an eighteen-foot leg span, literally weighed a ton, and was covered in yak hair, sisal, and hemp fibers, which are also used in broom-making.

Hagrid hid his giant half-brother, **Grawp**, in the forest for safety. Grawp seemed to develop a crush on Hermione.

Artificial lichen and moss, made from colored sawdust, were glued to the trees—on their north sides, of course!

Harry, Ron, and Hermione, along with Dolores Umbridge, encountered a herd of unfriendly centaurs in *Order of the Phoenix*.

For *Order of the Phoenix*, the creature shop created a life-size **Thestral** with extended wings to make sure the designated forest area was large enough to house these mysterious creatures.

In *Deathly Hallows – Part 2*, Harry goes to meet his destiny with Voldemort, who successfully casts the Killing Curse on him.

DID YOU NOTICE?
The Thestral's movements to bend over and take (or reject) the treats were based on those of a giraffe.

QUIDDITCH PITCH

Quidditch is the most popular sport in the Wizarding World, and Hogwarts has an intense annual competition between its four house teams. The object of Quidditch is to score points by hitting a Quaffle through one of three hoops. Each team has seven players: three Chasers, two Beaters, a Keeper, and a Seeker.

Harry Potter becomes the youngest **Seeker** ever in *Sorcerer's Stone*. When a Seeker catches the Golden Snitch—which is worth 150 points—that ends the game. The walnut-sized **Golden Snitch** was designed with grooves that hold thin, sail-like wings.

Ron Weasley became **Keeper** in his sixth year. To make Rupert Grint appear clumsy while filming his tryout, the stunt team fired up to twenty Quaffles at him at a time to fluster him. On-screen, it looked as if Ron was untalented and out of control.

Beaters use short bats to knock heavy **Bludger balls** at the opposing team. The Quidditch costume featured an arm guard called a bay for protection as well as padded-leather leg guards and shoulder protectors. Helmets were added to the uniform in *Half-Blood Prince*, as the game became faster and fiercer.

When Harry is hit by a rogue Bludger and makes a crash landing in *Chamber of Secre* he believes his right arm is broken. Gilderoy Lockhart tr to cure him with ***Brackium Emendo***, but the spell ends up removing Harry's bones!

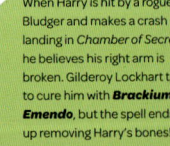

Rain goggles and water-repellent nylon robes were worn to combat the rainy weather in *Prisoner of Azkaban*. As if the weather alone wasn't tough enough while playing, the Dementors assigned to guard Hogwarts surrounded Harry, who lost consciousness and fell from his broom.

DID YOU NOTICE?

Quidditch is played in the air, so viewing stands for fans are set atop towers. The wooden towers feature wind-blown banners and heraldic designs in the four house colors. The towers are important to the films for another reason: The best way to show speed is to pass something.

Luna Lovegood showed support for her Gryffindor friends in *Order of the Phoenix* by wearing a lion-shaped hat.

Harry's **Nimbus 2000 broom** was jinxed by Professor Quirrell during a game in *Sorcerer's Stone*, so Hermione saves him with the *Lacarnum Inflamari* charm. When he tries to catch the Snitch, Harry tumbles off his broom—and catches the Snitch in his mouth!

INSIGHT
EDITIONS
PO Box 3088
San Rafael, CA 94912
www.insighteditions.com

Find us on Facebook: www.facebook.com/InsightEditions
Follow us on Twitter: @insighteditions

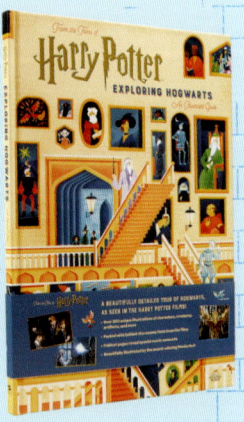

Library of Congress Cataloging-in-Publication Data available.

ISBN: 978-1-68298-684-4

Written by Jody Revenson
Illustrations by Studio Muti

Publisher: Raoul Goff
VP of Licensing and Partnerships: Vanessa Lopez
VP of Creative: Chrissy Kwasnik
Associate Art Director: Ashley Quackenbush
Design Support: Nancy Huynh
Product Lead: Nicole Crncich
Editorial Assistant: Elizabeth Ovieda
Production Associate: Andy Harper

Discover even more magic in the complete *Harry Potter: Exploring
Hogwarts: An Illustrated Guide*, available now at your local bookstore.

REPLANTED PAPER

Insight Editions, in association with Roots of Peace, will plant two trees for each tree used in the manufacturing of this book.
Roots of Peace is an internationally renowned humanitarian organization dedicated to eradicating land mines worldwide
and converting war-torn lands into productive farms and wildlife habitats. Roots of Peace will plant two million fruit and nut
trees in Afghanistan and provide farmers there with the skills and support necessary for sustainable land use.

Manufactured in China by Insight Editions

10 9 8 7 6 5 4 3

IN MEMORANDUM

Sadly, some members of the Wizarding World have passed away since the fini sh of Harry Potter's screen story. Thes e include
actor Richard Harris, whose Dumbledore made us all feel loved and safe; Stephenie McMillan, set decorator for all eight
film s; and actor Alan Rickman, who brought the always-intriguing Severus Snape to the screen. We raise our wands in
tribute to these talented people who brought their magic to the Harry Potter film s.